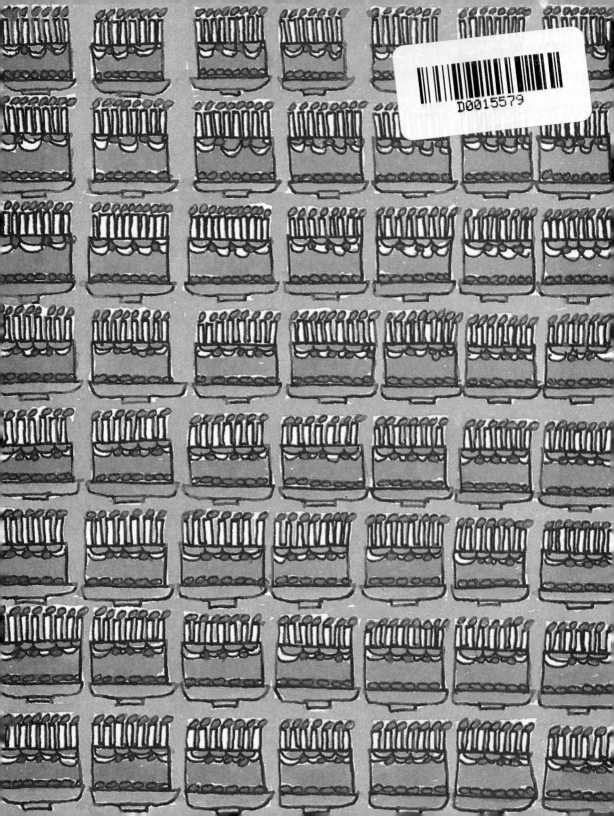

HENRY'S IMPORTANT DATE

by Robert Quackenbush

PARENTS MAGAZINE PRESS · NEW YORK

For Piet
and Margie

A Parents Magazine READ ALOUD AND EASY READING PROGRAM® Selection.

Library of Congress Cataloging in Publication Data
Quackenbush, Robert M.   Henry's important date.
SUMMARY: Due to circumstances beyond his control,
Henry arrives at Clara's birthday party just before
he thinks it will end.
|1. Time—Fiction| I. Title.
PZ7.Q16Hf   [E]   81–5026
ISBN 0–8193–1067–0   AACR2
ISBN 0–8193–1068–9 lib. bdg.

On the way to his friend Clara's birthday party, Henry the Duck got caught in traffic.

The traffic jam got worse and worse.
Henry did not want to be late
because he had Clara's birthday cake.
But the party was to start
at two o'clock.
And it was already
ten minutes to two.

At five minutes to two,
Henry saw a parking space
and began parking his car.
He thought that if he ran
to a quieter street
he would find a taxi
to take him to the party.

At exactly two o'clock,
Henry's car was parked.
Then he remembered that
the birthday cake was inside.
So were his keys!
He had locked the keys
and the cake inside the car!

At eight minutes after two,
Henry tried to pry open a window.
The window broke!
"Stop in the name of the law!"
called a police officer.
He thought Henry was a car thief.
So Henry showed the officer his license.
It said, "Henry the Duck."
The policeman let him go.

At twenty minutes after two
Henry ran to get a taxi.
But every one was full.

When a bus came along at two thirty,
Henry decided to take it.
He climbed aboard and
heaved a sigh of relief.
At last, he was on his way
to Clara's party.

But suddenly, at twenty minutes to three,
the motor sputtered and then stopped.
Henry waited and waited
for the bus to go again.

Henry wondered if he would
ever get to Clara's party.
The party would be over
by five o'clock.
And it was already
fifteen minutes to three!

At three o'clock,
the driver opened the bus doors.
"Everybody off!" he said.
"This bus is out of order."
Henry went to call Clara
to say he was on his way.
But he couldn't find a phone.

At twelve minutes after three,
Henry decided that the only way
to get to Clara's was to run.
But as he went tearing
down the street,
he bumped into a shopper
carrying a lot of packages.

Henry helped the shopper
pick up her packages
at twenty minutes past three.
Then he ran on with his own.
The shopper thought Henry
had one of her packages.
"Stop, thief!" she cried.

A crowd began chasing Henry
and caught up with him
at twenty-five minutes after three.
A police officer was called.
It was the same one as before.

At three thirty,
Henry opened the package
to show that it was his.
When the shopper saw the cake,
she said she was sorry
about the mistake.
Once again, the policeman
let Henry go.
Henry ran as fast as he could.

At ten minutes to four,
Henry got to Clara's
apartment house.
He jumped on the elevator
and pushed the button
to Clara's floor.
But half way there,
the elevator got stuck.

Henry pushed the bell for help.
A mechanic came to help him
at four o'clock.

At four thirty, Henry
was out of the elevator.
He raced up eight floors
to Clara's apartment
and rang the bell.
Clara opened the door.

"Happy birthday, Clara," said Henry.
"I'm sorry I'm late."
"Late?" asked Clara, surprised.
"But, Henry…

my birthday is not until tomorrow!"

ABOUT THE AUTHOR

Robert Quackenbush's last name means "duck in the bush" in Dutch. It was originally given to one of his ancestors who was a duck farmer in Holland a long time ago. So it is not surprising that Mr. Quackenbush is the creator of Henry the Duck, who first appeared in TOO MANY LOLLIPOPS and then in HENRY'S AWFUL MISTAKE. Mr. Quackenbush got the idea for this latest story, HENRY'S IMPORTANT DATE, when his six year old son was learning how to tell time.

Mr. Quackenbush is the author/illustrator of more than 40 books and the illustrator of another 70. His artwork has been exhibited in leading museums across the U.S. and is now on display in the gallery he owns and runs in New York City. He also teaches painting, writing, and illustrating there. Robert Quackenbush lives in New York with his wife, Margery, and their son, Piet. They have a cat—but no ducks.

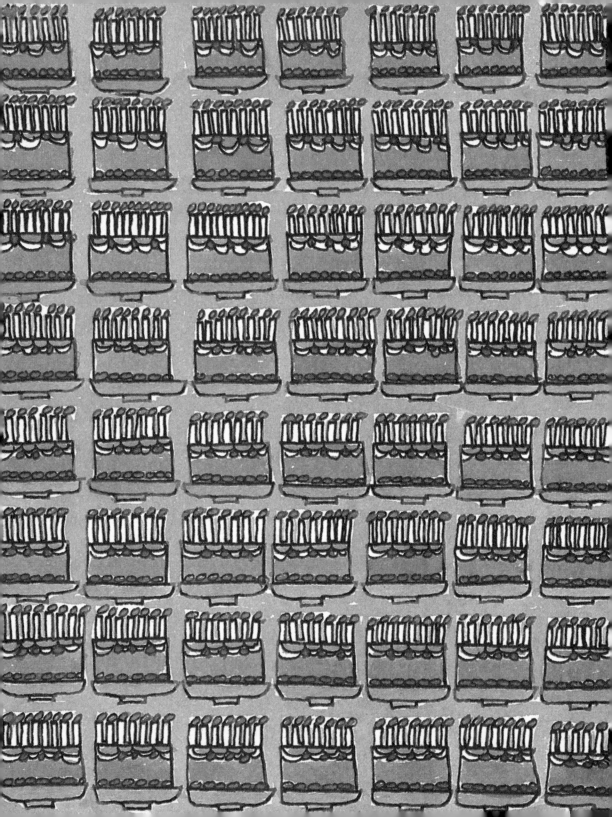